# the CIRCLES ALL AROUND US

WRITTEN by
BRAD MONTAGUE

ILLUSTRATIONS by
BRAD and KRISTI MONTAGUE

Dial Books for Young Readers

For all the kids
making the world
better right where
they are

DIAL BOOKS FOR YOUNG READERS

An imprint of Penguin Random House LLC, New York

First published in the United States of America by Dial Books for Young Readers,
an imprint of Penguin Random House LLC, 2021

Text copyright © 2021 by Brad Montague • Illustrations copyright © 2021 by Brad & Kristi Montague

Dial & colophon are registered trademarks of Penguin Random House LLC.

Visit us online at penguinrandomhouse.com.

Library of Congress Cataloging-in-Publication Data is available.

Manufactured in China • ISBN 9780593323182

7  9  10  8  6

Design by Jennifer Kelly • Text hand-lettered by Brad Montague
The artwork for this book was creating using both analog and digital elements.

We begin by drawing a circle

on the ground along each shoe.

A safe little place
for just one person.

Nobody in this
circle but you.

You could keep that circle closed
to everyone but yourself ...

but that would be like a library
with just one book on the shelf.

so let's draw a bigger circle

for you and your family to share.

Now you see what
all can happen

in a circle
full of care.

It becomes a happier circle

as more loved ones come to stay.

And wouldn't it be even better
if all your friends could come and play?

So you stretch and draw your circle
even bigger than it's been

and let a few more people know
they're welcome to come in.

In the circles all around us
everywhere that we all go

there's a difference we can make
and a love we can all show.

Yet, there are still so many outside the circle
who are different in all they do!

Though it feels slightly uncomfortable...

we draw a bigger circle
for them too!

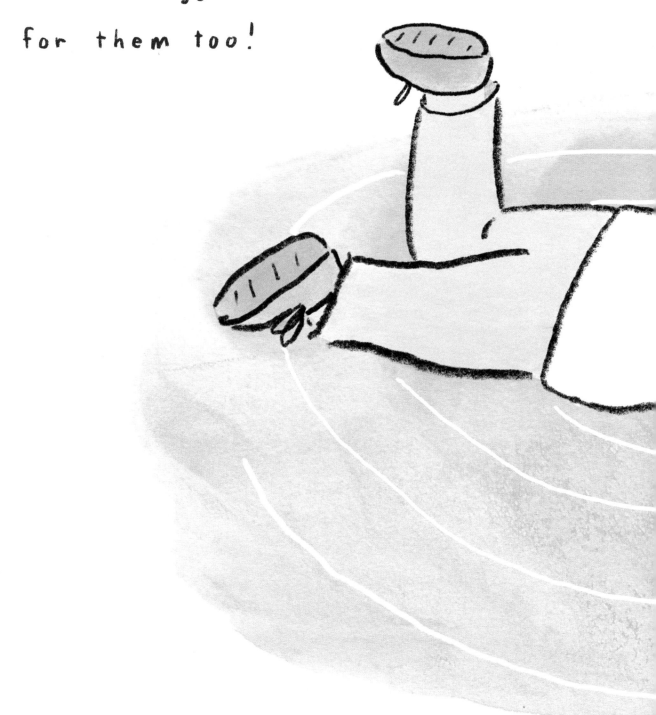

It doesn't mean the circle is easy.

It can get harder the more we share.

But wonderful things can happen

FRIENDSHIP DONUTS!

when love is known and felt everywhere.

As time passes, our eyes open.
We see others we really care for.

And that's when we ask ourselves,
well, what's this circle really there for?

So let us create bigger circles
all around us for the rest of our days.

in the circles all around us...

Let our caring ripple out in a million little ways.

In the circles all around us
everywhere that we all go

there's a difference we can make
and a love we can all show.

As our circles grow and grow

and we watch them wonder-eyed...

remember the first circle started
with just the love you hold inside.